Copyright ©

ISBN: 978-1-4710-3149-.
Matt Shaw Publications

All rights reserved. This book or any portion thereof may not be reproduced or used in any manner whatsoever without the express written permission of the publisher except for the use of brief quotations in a book review.

The characters in this book are purely fictitious.

Any likeness to persons living or dead is purely coincidental.

www.mattshawpublications.co.uk

With thanks to the following supporters of my work:

Steven Wexler, Gary Harper, Bernard Galpin, Amelia Sutherland, Karen Thomas, Jessica Shelly, Steve Chappo, James Herrington, Jean Kelly, Renee Luczynski, Cat Goy, Sharen Womack, Cipher66, Jennifer Brooks, Adam Searle, Mary Kiefel, Lucy Desbrow, Jill Rogers, Jacquetta B, Sophie Harris, Kristy Lytle, Melissa Potter, Jacqui Saunders, Nigel Parkin, Amber Chesterton, Billy Smith, Chris Peart, Jon Vangdal Aamaas, Peter Le Morvan, Gemma De-Lucchi, Julie Shaw, Marie Shaw, John Burley, George Daniel Lea, Donna Cleary, Lex Jones, Joanna Taylor, Karla Rice, Scott Tootle, Louise Turner, Kevin Doe, Andiboo, Sue Newhouse, Karen McMahon, Joy

Boysen, Mason Sabre, Anna Garcia-Centner, Angela McBride, Debbie Dale, Kelly Rickard Jennifer Eversole, Cece Romano, Jennifer Burg Palfrey, Michele Fleming, Jessica Richardson

A massive, massive thank you for supporting my work and being a part of my Patreon page!

Want your name listed here?
www.patreon.com/themattshaw

CHAINED

MATT SHAW

Part One
An Unusual Relationship

1.

I didn't hear the vehicle pull up in my driveway. Surprising really given how loud the diesel engines tend to be but - there we go. The first I knew of its arrival was the slam of the truck's door and then the driver's heavy footsteps as he walked around the back of his wagon. The rear door itself creaked as it was pulled open thanks to well-worn hinges.

Without a word I got up from the living room sofa and walked into the hallway and towards the front door. There, I waited for the driver to rap upon my door. I never open my house up until I absolutely have to for I do not want them peaking in and seeing how I live my life. There's not much to hide, I just find it intrusive when they appear to be peaking into *my* life.

There's commotion outside as the driver unloads my grocery shopping from the rear of the truck. They place the boxes - filled with bags - onto the stony drive and, from there, mount them onto their sack-truck for easier transporting. With ear pressed to the wooden door, I listen as the sack-truck's wheels struggle to smoothy turn over the stones as the driver pushes, or pulls, my shopping up to the house. The wheels stop. There's a thud as he sets the sack-truck down. I move my ear away from the door. There's a knock.

So the driver doesn't think I have been standing there, listening to their struggles, I wait a couple of seconds before I unlock the top latch and pull the door open a crack. I never open it all of the way as there is no need.

I smile.

'Hello.'

'Shopping delivery for you.'

'That's great, thank you. Can you just pile it up by the door and…'

'Did you want a hand in with it?' the driver asked. A young man in his early twenties. I'm unsure whether he is paying his way through university with this shitty job or whether he is a drop-out from college, stuck in this role for the rest of his miserable life.

I started my sentence again in the hope that - this time - he would let me finish it. 'Can you just pile it up by the door and be on your way? I'll bring it in myself, thank you.'

'Sure you don't want a hand?'

'Please. Just by the door is fine.'

I do hate to repeat myself. If people listened the first time, *really* listened that is, then I wouldn't have to waste my breath multiple times and get irritated. Still, the way he failed to grasp my simple instructions suggests to me that he *isn't* paying his way through university. Instead he is stuck in this job having dropped out of college… Because he is clearly an idiot.

'No substitutions today,' he said.

I didn't answer him as he started to unpack the plastic totes, setting the shopping-filled carrier bags down on the mat in front of my door. I do not ask him if he has a lot on. I do not ask him how his day is. I do not ask him whether he was looking forward to the weekend. To me, he is a non-entity.

If didn't take him long to empty the bags from the totes onto the drive. I'm glad. Even with the door open this tiny little crack, warm air is still escaping from my humble abode.

'If I can just get a signature please,' he said as he pulled an electronic device from where it was clipped to his belt. He handed the machine to me and I pulled it through the crack and into my house so that I could sign it easier. The screen is scratched and there is evidence of some bright spark having tried to sign it with ink before now. I despair but I remain silent as I use the plastic (inkless) stylo to scribble my name. Still silent, I pass the signed device back through the crack and into his waiting hands.

'Thank you,' he said. He clipped it back to his belt and collected his now empty totes from the floor. He stacked them back onto the trolley. 'Well, have yourself a good day,' he said.

I said nothing.

I watched as he dragged the trolley back to the rear of his van. There, he lifted the totes in one and slid them onto the vehicle before doing the same with the trolley. He didn't give me, or my house, a second glance as he returned to the driver's seat. There was a slight pause - no doubt he is looking to where he is headed next - and then the engine spluttered to life. Another slight delay - no doubt he is setting up his sat nav system - and I watched as the supermarket-branded vehicle pulled away from my drive.

'Bitch!' I called back into the house as soon as the truck was out of sight. 'Help.'

There was movement from the living room as she pulled herself up from the sofa.

There was a clatter of metal on the wooden flooring and then a scraping sound - *metal being dragged and a clinking and clanking* - as she started towards the hallway. I watched for her. She appeared in the living room doorway. She looked tired and her hair was a mess from where she'd napped on the sofa.

'Shopping is here,' I told her.

I pulled the door open to reveal the shopping bags. She nodded and started towards me. The chain - one side cuffed to her ankle and the other to my own ankle - continued chinking against the wooden flooring.

'Did you get the bits I asked for?' she asked.

'You'll see when you help me in with it,' I told her. In the past I would have just given her a straight answer but then I've found she always moans about helping me, or she doesn't do is as quickly as I would like her to. By not giving her a straight answer I've found it gives her further incentive to help me in with the delivery (or whatever she is doing for me) without wasting her breath with pointless moaning and more dumb questions.

She reached my side. I nodded towards the bags and - without further instruction - she leaned down and lifted two from the deck. I did the same and then - together - we marched them down the hallway and towards the kitchen. The chain joining us clanking the entire way.

2.

There is about a month's worth of shopping on the kitchen sides, waiting for her to put it away. I empty the bags, she puts the goods away. That's the rule and it's only put it place because she is the one who cooks. Being in charge of the cooking, it's only fitting that she puts things away where she wants them and not where I think they would go. Rest assured if I was the one who did the cooking, I would put the shopping away and, again, it would be where I deemed suitable. There is nothing more than being in charge of your own domain only to have someone come in and clean up after you. They think they're going a good job of putting things away but - in reality - they're making a mess of it. By the time you come to grab whatever they moved, it's not where it should be. Of course, you then ask them where they put it and they deny ever seeing it. So, I don't touch stuff in the kitchen and she doesn't touch stuff in the garage.

Although, to be fair, there are other reasons I do not allow her near the tools hanging on the back wall of my garage space.

The last bag I emptied, on purpose, is the one which contained the bits that she asked for. I couldn't say for why I held it back. I guess I just woke up in one of those moods but, to be fair, she'd driven me to it with her constant moaning and nagging. Had it not defeated the whole point of all of this, I'm sure it would have been easier to just kill her. Certainly more peaceful for me. Still, can't think like that. I can't go putting such thoughts in my head.

She saw the items she'd asked for (mostly women's products) and smiled. It's the first time I have seen her smile for as long as I can remember. I haven't missed her smile.

'Thank you,' she said.

'Just don't think I don't appreciate you,' I told her.

Given how black her eye was still, now seemed a good a time as any to remind her of that little fact: I do appreciate her. I might not always like her, and in the past I have hated her for various reasons but - I do appreciate her. Sometimes. I don't expect her to say anything remotely nice back. Her kinder words are few and far between - hence the black eye. I just wish she'd learn to respect me so we wouldn't even need conversations whereby I remind her how I truly feel for her. Or the other conversations where I remind her that - despite what she thinks of me - this is *her* fault.

She made all of this happen.

The final item to set down on the side was kept back from one of the earlier bags I'd gone through, and quickly pocketed for the right moment. Now was a good time, I figured. Instead of setting this one idly on the side, I held it out for her. When she stopped moving things from point a through to point b, she noticed me standing there like a wally.

'What's that?' she asked.

'An apology.'

She held her hand out and I put the item in her palm.

A small pot of her favourite foundation.

'Should cover up your bruise,' I told her.

She smiled but it wasn't a smile of genuine affection, or even gratitude. It - I don't know - seemed almost gleeful in its expression.

'What's the matter?' She asked, 'Feeling guilty?'

'I just thought…' I didn't know what to say. I thought she would have been a little more - I don't know - grateful? This shit was expensive and I didn't have to buy it. I just thought… Sometimes women like to make themselves look pretty and it's hard to do that with a shiner. I thought I was doing the right thing by her. And, yes, in truth - it's pretty ugly to look at. For the last week, I've had to fuck her in doggy or get her to ride me in reverse cowgirl.

Just as well missionary was never really my thing.

'Well?' She pushed me, clearly wanting to know what I *just thought*.

'I just thought you might have liked it,' I told her.

'Oh, so you're not sorry then?' Her left eyebrow raised. Her question was a direct challenge. I knew what she wanted to do. She wanted to push my buttons. She wanted to get a reaction because she knew - when I did go overboard - it ate at me for ages afterwards. A whole night of grovelling and apologising and promising it wouldn't happen again despite the fact we both knew I couldn't make such a promise.

'I've already apologised,' I reminded her.

She had nothing to say to that.

'What do you say to a woman with two black eyes?' I asked her. She didn't answer me. 'Nothing you haven't said twice before.' She looked at me blankly. 'Too soon?'

'I need to use the bathroom,' she said.

3.

I'm standing in the hallway, as still as I can so I don't accidentally yank the chain - and her in the process - whilst she is trying to do her business. Toilet-time used to be a cause for embarrassment for the both of us. I didn't like going with her listening and, she didn't like it when I was standing close.

'Can we remove the chain, just for this?' she once asked.

Her request was met with a resounding 'no'.

Now it's easier. Even now I get to listen to her tinkle whilst mentally humming *Raindrops keep falling on my head* as she does so. I sometimes wonder if she is doing the same in her own mind. I quietly smiled to myself - we've come a long way since having to turn the tap on as a way of encouraging our bodies to relax enough to let it flow.

The chain moved slightly across the floor from where she moved within the bathroom.

A second later and a flush of the chain drowned out the sound of the metal scraping across the wooden floorboard. Only when the toilet's loud flush quietened did I hear that she was running the tap water, no doubt washing her hands.

'You okay?' I asked.

Force of habit. I know she is okay. I just don't like the quiet between us when there is a door blocking my direct line of sight to her. I guess I get paranoid; I think she is up to no good or maybe trying to get away. Not that she can. The chain won't come away from her ankle without some real heavy-duty power tools or the key. She has no access to the tools and, not that she knows this yet, I can't recall what I did with the key.

The tap water stopped and - a couple of seconds later - she emerged from the bathroom shaking her hands dry. I bite my tongue. She knows I do not like it when she does that. It's unnecessary water marks on the wooden floor which are easily prevented if she'd just use the towel that hangs on the rail.

'I'm fine.'

I smiled - an act which, in itself, I am sure would have annoyed her given that she'd have *wanted* a reaction from not drying her hands properly.

'Ready to go back downstairs?' I asked.

She responded by leading the way. The chain scraping on the floor between us.

'Careful down the stairs.'

We have been tethered together for a good few weeks now and we are both used to the chain which binds us but - even so - I always find myself telling her to be careful. And to think that once upon a time she accused me of not caring.

Silently I followed behind her as she led the way down the stairs, the ground floor hallway and into the kitchen at the far side of the house. There, to avoid being in the way, I took a seat at the kitchen table as she started to put the shopping away.

'What did you want for dinner?' she asked.

I would have liked to have believed that her question was one out of politeness; an offer to cook a meal I actually wanted as opposed to what she *thought* I would have wanted. It wasn't though. She had done this to me a couple of times now. I say what I want and she makes a point of cooking something entirely different because that is the kind of cunt she is.

'Whatever you fancy.' I told her, 'I'm easy.'

She didn't say a word as she continued putting the shopping away before attempting to make a start on dinner.

She treats me like I am the bad person in this relationship but I'm not. If anything it is *me* who is the victim.

Part Two
Dinner

4.

I'm a few people away from being served my daily lunch of *shit in a tray* despite knowing whether there'll even be any food waiting for me. There's plenty to go around but - they don't like to serve me. Regardless, like a good member of this society, I queue daily in the "hope".

Hope? Funny to think of anyone being hopeful for this when it does finally get spooned onto my dinner tray. Animals eat better than we do in here but then that is how the majority of them are regarded: Animals. Despite what they say about me though, I'm not one of them. Furthermore I shouldn't be in here but my words fall upon deaf ears and still they continue to torment me at every given opportunity. Sometimes their actions are stopped by the guards watching and - other times - the guards smile and look the other way.

Black eyes, broken ribs, broken fingers, a broken nose, various cuts and bruises - there is not a week where one of the days is not filled with pain of some description; be it mental or physical.

I still stand though.

I still queue.

Two away and none of the servers seem to be paying attention to the faces of those they dish up for. With any luck it will stay like that and I'll get my daily bread.

One away and my stomach turns at the sound of the mash potato splatting into the other guy's dinner tray. It's more water than potato by the looks of it and yet - still - my stomach rumbles in anticipation.

The man walks away and I move up with my tray held out. I don't look at the man serving us our food. Instead my eyes are fixed firmly to my tray. If I don't see him, he doesn't see me. That's how it works, right?

To my relief a splattering of wet mash slops into my tray with enough force to almost make me dropped the damn thing. That would have been sod's law... They allow me to eat today but then I go and drop the food anyway. Still with my eyes down, I turned and walked away from the serving area.

Next up is the challenge of finding somewhere to sit. There is a pecking order of who sits where and - sadly - I am at the bottom of it.

I can't sit on the right because my skin colour is wrong. I can't sit immediately on my left because I'm not affiliated with any gangs. The next rows are for people who have been here longer, most of whom hate me just because I am new and, therefore, unknown to them so I don't even bother heading for those either. Especially as I don't want them *trying* to get to know me. Not that I have done anything wrong but - like everyone else - they'll judge me before hearing me.

I walk to the back of the room. On the left there is a table with one person sitting on it and, on the right - a completely empty one.

I'm here for a while, apparently, and it would be nice to have one friend at least so I head for the left. I set my tray down opposite the stranger.

'That seat's taken,' he said. With a frown, I slid my tray across to the next placement but he said again, 'That seat is taken too.'

I got the hint loud and clear and moved across to the empty table. I sat down, half-expecting someone to shout at me for sitting here but - thankfully - no one did. For now, at least, they were leaving me be.

I looked to the meal and - again - my stomach rumbled. Feeling the deep growl from within, I'm not sure as to whether this was still anticipation for what it was about to receive or whether it was fear. A little voice in the back of my mind whispered that, *it'll be a night on the cold steel rim of the cell's seatless toilet if you eat this.*

Need to eat.

With the plastic spoon, I shovelled up the first dollop of shit. The benefit of it being "slop" is that there is very little need to chew. Get it in your mouth, swill it around a little to break it up and then swallow it the fuck down before you get a real taste of it.

5.

'What's wrong?' she asked from across the dinner table. I looked up from staring at the meal and saw that her eyes were fixed on me. Her eyebrow raised; quizzical. 'You're not eating,' she pointed out.

'Yes I am,' I told her despite not having taken a single bite of what she'd so "lovingly" prepared. I looked back to the dinner. The sausages looked okay, if a little on the undercooked side, and the peas... Well, you can't exactly fuck up the cooking of peas, can you? I'm not the best cook, I'm not even a good cook come to think of it and yet even I can manage peas. The gravy was thick too, just how I like it with my bangers. But the mash potato on the side... Unwanted memories raced through my mind, mangling my thought processes. 'What happened to the potato?' I asked.

'They're mashed.'

I'm sure I had told her about the mash I'd been forced to eat. I'm fucking positive. Was she doing this on purpose to try and upset me? Even after the disagreement last time and how *that* ended?

'Mashed?' I repeated.

These things were nuked. Had I not watched her making everything, I would have sworn blind that she'd swapped them out for a packet of instant mash; that shit powder whereby you "just add water" to get the "perfect" mash potato.

'Is there a problem?' she asked.

I know she is trying to push my buttons. I feel like she does it on purpose in order to provoke a reaction and - more than that - I know exactly the reaction she is looking for.

'No,' I told her.

Without another word I cut one of the sausages up before stabbing it with my fork. In my head it wasn't the sausage I was stabbing her rather her eye instead. With the sausage stuck, I swirled it around the gravy and then dunked it into the mash before putting it into my mouth. I clamped my lips shut around the food and pulled the fork away from my mouth. I started to chew slowly with my eyes fixed on hers.

'It's good,' I said after I swallowed. 'Thank you.'

As I went to cut away a second piece of sausage, she too resumed eating. In fairness it wasn't that bad. It was just that the watery look of it reminded me of back then.

As I forked in the second mouthful I realised that whilst she looked as though she were eating - nothing was actually going in her mouth. Instead she was simply pushing it around the plate. No doubt she's upset her reaction wasn't better from me but... I swallowed the second mouthful down... This is actually quite nice. There's something very homely about sausage, mash, peas and thick gravy on a cold day. Reminds me of my childhood in a way.

'You're not hungry?' I asked.

She didn't answer me. She didn't even look. She just carried on pushing one of the sausages around her plate as though it were a toy.

'You get the nutritional value by eating it,' I told her sarcastically.

Immediately she set her knife and fork down either side of her plate. Her eyes didn't come away from the meal which had her so engrossed though.

'How long are we going to do this for?' she asked.

I set my knife and fork down too.

'You know the answer to that,' I told her.

Other than the ticking of an old clock, which hung on the dining room wall, there was a moment's silence.

'If you're done eating,' I told her, 'we can get an early night.'

6.

Our days are mostly spent bickering despite my best intentions not to have *every* day follow a similar pattern. It just can't be helped. She doesn't understand why I am doing this to her and even though it makes perfect sense in my head, I struggle to explain it in a way she would get it.

Despite the bickering - and occasional bruise - our days are falling into a steady routine though. We get up at the same time every day, we would take it in turns in the bathroom... Whilst one is washing, the other is waiting outside. We would then have breakfast and then potter around the house doing chores, watching television, occasionally playing a game of cards. I would use the Internet whilst she would watch.

With regards to the computer she is, of course, not permitted to use the machine. As a result she must turn around each time it is loaded up so she cannot see the password I put in. If I think there is a chance she may have guessed it, or even attempted to sneak a look - I would have changed it.

Our conversations were mostly small talk. I would ask her something, or point something trivial out, and she would (if I was lucky) acknowledge it. She would then say something to me and I would answer her. Occasionally conversation would turn to the chains and for how long they needed to remain. It was a question I had answered her before yet - it was a question which would repeatedly crop up over and over. I answered it straight once, and only once. She would also bring her family up from time to time too.

'Can I at least let them know I am okay?' she'd ask.

The answer was always the same. A simple - and straight forward - *no*. So simple and straight forward, in fact, that I was often surprised when she would repeat the question a few days later as though my answer would have changed.

It never did.

Our days continued.

She would prepare our meals whilst I would sit, watching. I would then clean then up whilst she sat watching. Today's meal of bangers and mash left a fair bit to scrape off into the garbage sack but, usually, the meals were adequate enough for the both of us to have mostly cleared the plates which meant washing up was the breeze it usually was.

'This was a waste,' I told her as I finished scraping the last of the plates over the garbage sack. The sack itself stunk from foods already discarded which had started to fester in the bottom of the bag. A grim smell of rotting meat which - if the weather were warmer - would no doubt attract the flies. 'I told you I don't want to be wasting food like this. If you're not hungry, you shouldn't cook as much.'

This isn't the first time we had had this conversation either. Whenever conversations of the outside world come to be at the dinner table - she is quick to find her appetite fade which is why I usually put a radio on during meal time. Something to kill the silence. This evening I had forgotten and - as a result - paid the price with wasted food. On a positive note, it was sausages and mash and not a pricey piece of steak which I have been known to purchase in on special occasions.

'When I was locked up,' I told her, 'I was forced to eat all kinds of fucked up shit. Not fit for pigs. Yet here I feed you well...' This too was a conversation we'd had before. 'I've told you before - you make me waste food like this - I'll quite happily replicate the food I'd had.' I laughed to myself. 'Even I can't fuck up cooking that crap.'

'I'm sorry,' she said.

I turned to her without a word. I could tell from her expression that she wasn't sorry in the slightest. She wasn't even sorry when I had blackened her eye or winded her. She just stood right back up and looked straight back into my eyes with this very same defiant look she has now. She does it all on purpose. She wants to make my life here as hard as she believes I am making it for her.

She thinks her life is hard? I squirt lubricant inside of her to offer at least a little comfort but - yeah - she thinks her life is hard.

Part Three
Romance Is Dead

7.

I remember the first time I penetrated her. We didn't fuck, despite both of us feeling pent up and frustrated. We made love. If it had been a film, I would have imagined there to be candles flickering, barely lighting the room. I would have pictured the curtains blowing in a gentle breeze from the open windows. Soft music playing in the background, perhaps barely drowning out our soft moans as my hard cock slid into and out of her wet pussy. Her hands on my hips, pulling me into her deeper with each thrust forward of my body. The way we kissed, our tongues gently exploring one another's mouth. Our eyes locked - seemingly both enjoying watching the satisfaction on our partner's face as we both sought to give the other the climax they yearn for.

Even when she rode me, me on my back and my hands on her hips now, it was softer than anything you'd see in a porn film. A gentle rocking back and forth and sliding up and down on my member. The way her she arched her back and her body shuddered as she came. How breathless she sounded and yet her determination to keep riding me until I too came hard into the rubber that I was wearing.

When we were both done, we collapsed in one another's arms. We just laid there, silent for a while as we both enjoyed the post-orgasm feeling. I felt as though she were the one despite the fact she'd a husband waiting for her at home. I *wished* she were the one and it took my all not to tell her that I loved her.

I find myself flush at the thought of all of that. It's a million miles from how I usually am with women but she had been different from the moment I had met her in the bar. She wasn't a quick pick-up, despite that being exactly what I set out for that night. She was different to the rest of the women

I'd been with. It's hard to explain. Still - thinking back to how we made love... I still cringe. I still feel weird about it as though my friends would have mocked me had they known how the evening went. No rough hard fucking that night, which we usually brag about... *Different*.

A connection! That's what I felt that night! The word was on the tip of my tongue. A connection. That's what we had. Or so I thought.

Anyway.

Tonight - and the nights since the first - are different again. We don't make love. For her - she doesn't do anything now but lay there with her eye closed. Sometimes she cries I get on top and just fuck her hard and fast until I cum. Her tears do not bother me. I don't care about her enjoyment. I don't care whether she is in the mood or feeling the moment. *They* didn't care about me. *They* just did as they pleased and then pushed me to one side when *they* were done. Fair is fair; she gets the same treatment. I fuck her like *they* fucked me: Me on my front, them on my back. She is on her front. I am on her back. She should be grateful I at least go in her cunt.

I pulled my cock out and, with it, dragged a sample of my ejaculated semen. Not the first time I have pulled out, only to be followed by a little more of "me" trickling out straight after. Nor is it the first time I have wondered whether she was as repulsed at feeling my semen leak out of her as I was when I felt *them* leak out of me. She had one load in her. Even if it were a heavy one, it was still *one* load. I had multiple loads.

I rolled onto my side, facing away from her. She didn't move from her spot on the bed. Unlike the first time we made love, there were no pleasantries, there were no kind words. No cuddling... There was nothing. I'll be asleep soon enough. She knows we need to be up at the usual time tomorrow so I doubt she'll try and keep consciousness for long.

We do not wish one another a good night.
Let's see what tomorrow brings.

8.

The shower water cascaded over me, running down my body. A welcome warmth which washes away the coldness of the cell and the grime that I feel I sleep in. In here I like to close my eyes and pretend I am at home. I like to imagine that I am standing in my own bathroom with an array of soaps to my side that I can choose from, depending on my mood, as opposed to the white bottle of generic "body wash". I like to imagine that I am alone and not surrounded by a number of other men; all of whom standing in varying shapes and sizes but with an equal amount of *bad attitude* amongst them.

I try not to pay attention to the people sharing the showers with me. One wrong look in this place can lead you to a stay in the infirmary and - of those overnighters - I have had my fair share already and do not need more. If I have to be here, even though I protest my innocence until I am blue in the face, then I want my time to be spent in the quiet of my own cell. Well - as quiet as it can be for, even though they could be confined to their own cells, they still manage to find a way to pay me a visit when their mood suits.

The showers.

As much as I love the warmth of the water and cleaning away the muck, I try and be as quick as I possibly can in here. Long enough to get clean and a short enough trip as to avoid confrontation.

I reached for the taps and turned them counter-clockwise, killing the flow of water in the process. *Get in, get out.*

I turned for my towel but instead of finding the shitty fabric of the prison-issued towel I was met with a heavy left fist straight to my face. A hard blow which knocked me onto my arse down on the tiled, puddled flooring of the shower room. With my nerves on fire I looked up to see the room near enough empty of the other occupants. Instead, standing over me, a group of men who'd made their hatred obvious of me from the day I moved onto the wing.

All naked.

All grinning.

Behind them a watching guard stepped from the room. He closed the heavy metal door as he left.

*

Morning was here yet again. A morning which had started okay until she'd made the announcement that she wanted a shower.

Now, sitting here on the hallway floor, listening to the shower's water emptying over her and into the tub she was standing in - I cannot help but remember all that I had been through.

I would like to say it wasn't her intention to bring these memories to the forefront but - there's a part of me which always thinks the worst of her. I just hope that she's quick. Unless - although I only shot my load last night and I'm not really in the mood for it - maybe I should give her the same shower treatment that I'd received when I was doing my time?

Thinking how I feel now and the rage brewing within, I'm surprised that I haven't already gone in there after her and shown her another side of what I had put up with.

I looked to the crack in the doorway. It was wide enough for the chain to fit through but it wouldn't take much to push my way in, even if she has tried to block the door from opening any further.

My heart skipped a beat at the thought of kicking the door in and fucking her. The heart skipped a beat but - luckily for her - the cock didn't.

From within the bathroom, the shower stopped. Movement from beyond the door and the chain moved as she must have stepped out of the tub. She'd better have put something down on the floor to stop the drips of else there'd be trouble.

'You going to be much longer?' I asked.

In fairness she hadn't even been ten minutes yet. Even so - I am sick of sitting here. I am sick of remembering *my* time in the showers. I am sick of *her*.

There was no vocal answer but the door opened. She was standing there with a towel wrapped around her head and another tied just beneath her armpits to hide her modesty.

As she stepped out of the bathroom, she turned immediately right and headed for the bedroom to get dressed. Before the chain had a chance to drag me, or trip her, I jumped up and followed up to the doorway where I stopped.

I've seen her naked. I've cum inside of her. Even so - inside the bedroom - she gets privacy to get dressed, just as I do when I put my clothes on.

Part Four
The Morning After

9.

The morning after we fuck is always strained. It's not as bad as the first time I forced myself on her but - it's still not great. Tough really. Just one of those things that we have to live with I guess because, I'm not going to stop just because she wants me to.

I wanted *them* to stop but they didn't.

In the kitchen, she put a bowl down in front of where I was sitting. Filled with cornflakes and a splash of milk, just the way I like it. She sat opposite me but with no bowl for herself.

'You're not eating?' I asked.

'Not hungry.'

I nodded. I can't force herself to eat. If she wants to starve herself then that's down to her. I still won't take the chain off and if she loses too much weight - or looks to be losing too much weight - I'll simply tighten it so that there's still no room for movement.

To prove I didn't care if she starved herself I added, 'More for me, hey...'

'Why are you doing this to me?'

Her question was straight out of left-field. We had covered this ground time and time again - even though I'd only ever given her the straight answer the first time she asked. I figured I had explained it adequately enough the first time and didn't want to waste more time on ground already covered.

'You know.'

'Why don't you just kill me?' she asked.

I couldn't help but smile. 'Life with me that bad?' The smile turned into a chuckle. 'Imagine a whole house full of people like me and most of them are treating you like dirt.' I paused long enough for her to contemplate that. 'Picturing it? That's nothing to what I put up with.'

'Just kill me.'

'I'm not a murderer. Just as I'm not a...'

'Please,' she cut me off. 'Please, just kill me.'

We had spoken of the same subjects again and again over the time we had spent together but this particular subject - me killing her - was all new territory.

I put the my spoon down on the wooden table and pushed the bowl away from myself. The cereal was ruined now. Even with a splash of milk, it's still quick for the cereal to become too soggy and remind me of the slop we'd be eating inside.

'You're pathetic,' I told her. I didn't want to shout at her. I didn't wait to raise my voice and get mad. I don't want to argue and for her to try and push my buttons to force my hand again. But at the same time she needed to be told. She needed to hear this; a conversation not yet had while in this house with me but one she needed to hear.

'Please...'

I continued, 'You're fucking pathetic. How long have we been here? A few months, if that. Have I said that I was going to kill you? No. Have I promised you your freedom? Yes. I've even given you the date of when you can go home. But instead of working towards that date - something which I never had - you just want me to kill you?' I paused a moment as she started to cry.

Crying isn't something she has done too much in front of me. No doubt it is because she thinks it would please me to see her in such a state. In fairness, it does make me a little happy but that is neither here nor there.

I told her again, 'You are fucking pathetic.' This time the sentence didn't escape my mouth with as much relish as the first time I'd said it though. This time is was spat out with the resurfacing of an old memory racing to the forefront of my imagination.

10.

Nights were the worst. The blackness and stillness of the cell. The dripping of a leaky tap in the sink attached to the far wall next to the steel toilet. The thin, itchy blanket which failed to keep me warm even on the hottest of nights. The voices in my head asking for why this was even happening and - worst of all - the calling from across the way. Hushed voices whispering my name through the darkness, telling me that I won't be here too long. People like me never are. These voices not promising me my freedom but rather threats against my life.

I quietly wept the first night I was there. The second night I struggled to be *as* quiet. The third night I laid awake, my eyes tearless, thinking about fashioning a noose from the blanket and wondering from where I could secure the other end in order to hang myself. They were thoughts I had on a few occasions but never once did I actually try and go through with it and despite wanting to die, I never actively looked for someone else to kill me.

*

'I don't want to do this anymore,' she said again as I stared, blankly, at her from across the kitchen table. Her words pulled me back to the present. 'Please - just let me go or kill me.'

'You think I wanted to go through what I went through? You think that was fun and games for me? You're here with me and while there might be some things you don't enjoy - trust me, you have got it fucking easy compared to what I had. Easy, I tell you.'

She sat there in silence but I could tell she didn't believe me. To her - I knew - this was the hardest thing ever asked of her. Pathetic. This is a walk in the park compared to what I had, not that she knows *everything* that I was put through. I don't hide things to protect her, or because I don't want her feeling bad. I hide certain things because -

well - I am ashamed of what they did to me. If I talk about it, it makes it all the more real. If I bury it, I can at least try and pretend it was nothing more than a nightmare.

I tried to change the subject in an effort to make her see that - whatever she is feeling now - this isn't actually that bad. 'You didn't hate me when you first met me,' I told her.

She laughed, although I'm not sure what the joke was.

'What?' I asked.

'You didn't chain me to you and keep me a prisoner when we first met.'

'No, you came back to mine willingly.'

The sarcastic smile faded from her face and the conversation dried up. A conversation killer if ever there was such a thing.

'In fact if memory serves me correctly, and please do say if I am wrong, it was even you who suggested coming back to my home... You know, when we first met...'

'I was drunk.'

'You were tipsy but you knew what you were doing.'

'Think things could have been different for us?' I asked. All this time together and - yet - this was the first time such a conversation had cropped up. I've often wondered though; how things *could* have been. Most of the time plagued by such thoughts as I lay on the thin mattress in my small cell.

She didn't answer me so I pushed her.

'What's the matter? Worried about offending me? I think we are past that, don't you?'

She hesitated over her words for a moment and, then, 'You were a bit of fun.'

'A bit of fun?'

'Yes. I'm sorry.'

I couldn't help but laugh at her apology.

'You're sorry about *that*? Okay. Well, it's nice to know I was at least fun. A shame though as I thought we were at the start of something new and exciting. But a bit of fun is better than nothing I suppose.' I added, 'A bit of fun right up until when your husband found out, hey?'

'There was a baby,' she said suddenly and with a change in her tone of voice. My heart skipped a beat.

Part Five
Innocence & Lies

11.

My hands were up in a defensive position as they surrounded me. One of them stepped forward and spat on me; a gross dollop of sucked-up saliva straight on my cheek where it proceeded to dribble down as the group laughed. I looked from face to face - none of them friendly. I looked beyond them for the guards but they'd already left, happy to leave *them* to whatever it is they have planned. Not that it takes a genius to figure out. They've spelt out their intentions quite clearly with, *we're going to fuck you up*.

I'd already decided not to fight back, although I know how to swing a punch. There's more of them than there is of me and it will only serve to make the beating I receive more severe. But that doesn't mean I won't try - again - to explain *my* side.

'I didn't rape her,' I told them.

'Of course not - just tripped and slipped inside, right?'

'I didn't rape her. We met at a bar. We went back to mine - her fucking choice…'

'Then what? You got there? She changed her mind? You fucked her anyway…'

'That's not what happened…'

The guy on the left swung the first punch. It connected hard to my jaw and snapped my head to the right with a loud click of my neck. The pain was instant but I didn't go down - just staggered. Before I regained my footing, I was pushed back to my original placement in the centre of the group by a guy on my right.

'She was married… I guess her husband found out and instead of losing her relationship she said I raped her…'

The group laughed. A punch came from the right. I staggered to the left and, again, was pushed back to the centre. There was no point talking. They weren't listening. Worse, every time I opened my mouth - there was a shooting pain straight from my jaw right up to my brain.

This wasn't the first time I had tried to explain what had happened and nor was it the first time my words had been ignored and I'd taken the beating given. It's not just the fellow inmates who don't believe me though. No one does. The judge didn't, the guards don't, even the nurses in the infirmary don't. To all of them - I am, and forever will be, a rapist.

To my *own* family - I am the monster she had me labelled as.

The next punch floored me but they still didn't leave me be. One of them lifted me to my knees and kept me there as I spat blood down my front. The others - for once in their life behind these walls - formed an orderly queue with fists at the ready.

In here rapists and kiddy-fiddlers are the lowest of the low. In here they are given the punishments most on the outside yearn to give but fear to do so for repercussions of the justice system. I look up to the next inmate in the "queue" and lock eyes to his. I hope that he can look into my eyes and see the truth. He raises his fist.

He can't see anything but her lies.

12.

I looked at her with... I don't even know the expression on my face right now. I've been punched more times than I care to remember and yet this was a true sucker-punch which has knocked me for six and, not for the first time, I am at a loss for words.

'You're lying,' I told her whilst trying to keep as cool and level-head sounding as possible. I said again, 'You are a *fucking* liar.' I couldn't help but to laugh. 'But then why am I shocked by that? You lied before. You're lying now. In fact - right from the moment we met you've been nothing but a fucking liar.'

She pulled my bowl of cornflakes away from where I'd left them in front of me. Then she took my spoon and started to eat them as though there wasn't a care in the world.

'I'm not lying,' she said casually, swallowing a mouthful of soggy flakes.

'I wore protection,' I told her. 'When I came, I did so in a fucking rubber...'

'Ever read the packet? They're not 100%.'

I didn't know what to say. I just sat there watching her as she continued to eat what was intended to be my breakfast. Then it clicked.

'I know what you're trying to do.'

'Oh you do? And what am I trying to do?'

'You're trying to make me mad. You're trying to make me angry enough that I snap and do something stupid. You're hoping that there'll be so much rage that I'll take it too far and kill you, as you originally asked.'

'Is that right?'

'Then for why bring it up now after all this time when you could have said something earlier? And where'd this baby go then? This magic fucking baby...'

She stopped eating a moment. Her eyes still locked to mine. 'You think I would want to keep it? I mean I could have said it was my husband's child but - why? Why would I want it? The baby of a rapist? Growing inside of me? No thank you.'

I slammed my fist down on the table hard enough to make her flinch. My insides were on fire as my red hot blood surged through my body. I even felt my damn face start to burn up as it flushed with anger.

She knows I didn't rape her just as I know there is not an aborted baby lying in the trash somewhere, sucked from her insides with a fucking vacuum.

There was a moment's silence between the two of us but neither looked away. The cruel words from her mouth and the way she was looking at me, I wanted to beat her to an inch of her life. An inch I would leave her with for she isn't going to die. She can serve her time just as I had served my time.

I told her again, 'I know what you're trying to do.'

'Then just do it.'

'I'm not a monster.'

'Everyone thinks that you are.'

I gritted my teeth and swallowed the hatred for her down and then - after a pause - I slowly smiled.

'What happened to your husband anyway? I noticed you weren't wearing your ring... He finally see you for what you are? A cheating piece of shit? He finally kick you to the curb with all of the other whores out there? Or is he inside now? Maybe he too was wrongfully convicted?'

She didn't say anything although I could tell from her face there was plenty left in her to say. Even so - she'd pushed me so I wanted to push her. That was how our relationship worked.

'Unless...' I teased.

I could tell from her face that she was worried where I was going with this. If I read her wrong and she wasn't concerned, she'd be a fool.

'Maybe you carried on living together for a little while longer, after I was sent to prison. Maybe it was him that changed? Every time he saw you - he saw me inside you... Not making love, like we did, but fucking you hard... Maybe he saw you crying out as I fucked you good and proper... Maybe he heard you begging him to get off and leave... Maybe he saw my face as I came deep in your pussy... Maybe he saw your pussy, ripped to shreds where I'd gone in dry - even though we both know you were fucking wet for it... Maybe he saw it all and couldn't cope? He didn't leave you though, did he? He didn't blame you. He wasn't mad at you. He blamed himself. He should have been there for you. He should have stopped me from attacking you. He wished he had caught me and that it hadn't been the cops who'd come knocking on my front fucking door... He failed you. The man of the house, your husband... The love of your fucking life... He failed you and - as a result - I violated you. I fucked you so hard and ruined you for him... Your husband, the failure... Is that what happened? Did you come home one day and find him swinging there from the attic rafters with a cord around his neck? You find him in the closed garage sitting in his car... A hosepipe leading from exhaust to a tiny crack in the window? His skin all blue, his eyes closed forevermore... Your dirty fucking lies not only ruin my life but his too?'

She started to cry.

I sat back, a smile on my face.

'Or maybe he just left because you're a vile cunt.'

The record looped back to the start as she asked me - once again - to just kill her.

'If you have finished eating my breakfast... I want to get onto the computer.'

Slowly she stood up and walked over to the kitchen sink carrying the bowl and spoon where - technically - I should have gone to wash it up. It's one bowl though so I do not feel as though there is an urgency to clean it despite an old conversation coming to mind from when we first came to be in this situation. She likes washing up done immediately so it isn't left to gather... Well, I like not being accused of a rape I had never committed.

Part Six
Online

13.

My computer is simplistic at best. A budget-range machine purchased with the sole intention of using it to get on the world wide web. I told the salesman that I only wanted it to surf the Net but - of course - he kept asking question after question after question. Do I want this program and that program? Programs that - to this day - I have no idea what they are used for. I said no to everything but he kept trying to push me until I threatened to just walk from the store. Then he changed tact and resigned himself to a smaller sale with less commission other than one which would earn him enough for a good night out. The final offer he made was for an anti-virus program and I am sure I surprised him when I'd said I *would* take that. It made sense, after all, especially as I was using the computer to scour various websites - some of which would most likely try and force downloads upon me. An anti-virus program made perfect sense.

As per the "rules", she turned away when I entered the computer's password onto the keyboard I'd purchased with the unit. Sometimes she would stay facing away, happy to occupy herself with a book from my extensive collection and - other times she liked to watch what I was doing over my shoulder. The latter I'm not sure why - I always felt like she was just torturing herself with being that close to connecting with people and still being unable to. I didn't point this out to her though. If she wanted to make things harder on herself, that was fine with me. I keep saying it: She has it much easier here with me than what I had to endure.

'You can turn around if you wish,' I told her.

Today was one of the days where she decided to keep herself busy instead. I waited for her to make herself comfortable with a book on a nearby seat as it irritated me to try and type whilst the chain pulled at my leg.

'Done?' I asked when she'd settled.

She didn't answer me. She merely opened the book and started to read. A cruel thought popped into my head; a little voice whispering that - as punishment - I should remove the back page when she isn't looking. I dismissed the idea as petty and turned back to the computer.

Online, I browse the various News sites for my local area. To find them all I needed to do was put in the name of the town along with the words "today's news" and - boom - pages of various sites. I never scroll past page one though. Page one is where the reputable news-sites are found. Beyond that most of the sites are random blogs run by people who believe in the existence of alien-life form and other whacky conspiracy theories. Good for a laugh, if you're desperate, but not good for reliable information.

I scroll the news first. Because I live in a quiet area there's never much of anything; the odd burglary, the occasional traffic accident and various townsfolk who are going out and about to try and raise money for charity. I'm not looking for any of this information though and I pay little to no attention to it. What I am seeking are reports of missing people. More particular, I am looking for news featuring her.

After the first week there were a few bits and pieces on her. They were mainly saying she'd vanished and it was out of character for her to do so. She'd left her home without her purse, money, cards, phone… She'd literally just vanished. People were urged to come forward with information if they'd seen her at all.

Of course, no one would be coming forward. No one knows anything. She literally disappeared from her life and I'd ensure she would stay "gone" until I was ready to let her go back out.

I'd gone to a lot of trouble to ensure this went smoothly.

14.

I would be a prime suspect in her disappearance had I acted on impulse and taken her soon after my release. I wanted to grab her. I wanted to put my plan into action. I wanted to go straight round to where I knew she lived and confront her for what had happened but - if I did - I would have been seen as being in the wrong and sent straight back to my little cell. Having just got out, the last thing that I wanted was to be turned around and sent straight back. I never want to go back. I never will.

I lived in the same town as her for a while and ensured I avoided going to where she'd initially met me. The last thing I wanted was to accidentally bump into her. I'm not sure of the protocol for letting victims know when the person who supposedly violated them is released from their sentence. To this day I still don't actually know if she was warned that I was back on the streets.

Jesus - even I am making it sound as though I am a criminal. I did nothing wrong but take a willing girl home and sleep with her.

A little over a year after being out of prison - I sold my home. It was a nice property and had earned me a good wage in rent while I was staying with Her Majesty but I knew I couldn't keep it as somewhere to live. I knew - if I had - the police would have come straight round while investigating her disappearance. So, yes, I sold it.

The timing of the sale was for two reasons: On the one hand it would make it look less likely as to me being involved and, on the other hand, I knew I wouldn't have been allowed to travel abroad for the first twelve months of my release anyway.

When the money had cleared into my bank, I paid them a visit and closed the account down. They'd tried to give me a cheque for the value of what was being kept by them but I insisted upon cash although - much to my frustration - it took them a few days to get it all prepared for me. So much for easy access to my money.

Of course they asked questions. They asked whether I was moving to another bank, unhappy with their services - all the usual rubbish. It was none of their business but I wanted everyone to know my story: I was moving abroad to start a new life. They seemed interested to know more and almost seemed jealous, like they wanted to pack up and come with me. I can't say I blamed them. This country seems to have changed in my time away unless of course it was always this shitty and my old character just saw less of the bad and more of the good? Who knows.

Before my plan was put into action, I used cash and fake identification to purchase the secluded property I live in now and I bragged of my "moving abroad" plans on the various social media sites I'd joined, since my release.

Just as the bank-teller was jealous, so were the few friends I had made online. All of them asking if they could come visit. Of course I said they could - as soon as I was settled in... These days hours online are spent scouring the news sites and also updating my social media accounts with pictures stolen from strangers' profiles or Google Image... *Check out this beautiful sunset, look at my view... blah blah...*

No one ever questions as to why I'm not in the pictures. They mostly just say they wish they were there too, or call me playful names because they're viewing the pictures on their office computer while stuck at work.

If only they knew the truth.

I navigated to my page and started uploading some new pictures I'd earlier found whilst browsing the net. She, meanwhile, continues to quietly read with only the occasional page-turn reminding me she is there.

It didn't take long to upload the pictures and - no sooner had the last one gone up - I turned the system off and turned slightly in my chair so that I could watch her. My mind was stuck - reminiscing - on our first night as a couple who'd be living together for the foreseeable.

Part Seven
Before

15.

After bragging of my move to another country, I remained in hiding in my new home for a couple of months before I ventured out to carry out my revenge. Because the property I'd purchased was so small, I had a lot left over from the sale of my previous home. I also had a fair amount of collected rent from where my home had been occupied while I was inside. Sure the money will not last forever but - being careful - it is possible to make it stretch. If my household was looked into though, I would definitely be told I was one of the poorer members of society living in this country. *On the bread-line*. Isn't that what they called it? It didn't matter though. We were never to leave the house and we didn't have anything to spend the cash on but the basics so - we didn't need lots of cash. We just needed budgeting and that was something I'd always been good at.

I'd taken her in the dead of the night. Stalking her home and waiting for the perfect opportunity - I saw her coming home late one night and, better yet, she was a little worse for wear, stumbling over her own feet. Despite the drink, when she saw me approach, it was safe to say she recognised me.

Before she'd a chance to scream, she was unconscious.

'What do you want?' she'd asked.

I remember how she looked, sitting on the floor close to where she was sitting now. No book in her hand back then though. Her eyes were streaming, her hair knotted and tangled, her clothes in disarray. She was a mess and yet - bizarrely - I still found myself attracted to her, even with the way she looked and what she'd put me through.

'My life back but that's an impossibility,' I replied.

I told her of my plans. She was going to stay chained to me for the same amount of time as I had spent locked behind bars. At the end of her "sentence", the chain would be removed, and she'd be allowed to leave. Her punishment, over.

She immediately broke down in floods of tears. She said that she'd tell people she'd lied to save her marriage. She told me that she was sorry, but it didn't matter. None of what she'd said that day mattered. The only words which mattered were the ones which had cost me my freedom and no matter what she said now - I would never get that freedom back again. Her words, back then, had forever changed my life and - now - they'd caused her life to change too.

Thinking back - what would have happened had I believed her though? What if I had let her go? She wouldn't have done as she'd promised. She would have told the police what *I* had done. She would have told them about the chain and my plans for us and - in the blink of an eye - I would have been incarcerated again. I mean, I was the one with the criminal record so - why wouldn't they believe what she was saying?

And she was the one with the record for lying so - why would I be stupid enough to have believed her?

She turned the page of her book and happened to glance up, catching me looking at her lost in thought.

'What?' she asked.

I stuttered a moment and - then - I confessed, 'That night we met and I took you back to mine... You know... I never once thought of you as a one-night stand. I didn't think of you as a conquest. If you recall, I tried calling you a few times after we met but you ignored my calls. For me it was never about the sex. I thought we had a connection and I thought we might have had a chance of, you know, *going* somewhere. As a couple, I mean.'

I have no idea where the confession had come from given my previous thoughts. Maybe it was the thought of still finding her attractive on the night I dragged her back here for the start of her punishment which made my brain spit it out. Whatever. It's out now. Can't take it back though. I wonder though… Will it get a confession from her too?

'You knew I was married,' she said coldly.

I shrugged. 'Marriages break up.'

'Hardly the foundation of a new and stable relationship though, is it?'

'Just because you don't have something with one man… All it would take is for another to make you realise that and, when that "other" man comes along… Doesn't mean you'd want to leave him too.'

She didn't say anything.

'We could have had something special,' I told her.

'You chained me up,' she said in a matter of fact tone which I couldn't help but to laugh at.

'You had me locked up.' I added, 'You think you have it bad here? Want to know what they did to me?'

Part Eight
Inside

16.

It hurt every time they first stuck *it* inside me. A sting as my tense sphincter muscles were forced open and unpleasantly stretched by their girth. It didn't matter that I let out a cry of pain. It didn't matter to them that I begged them to stop - still protesting that I wasn't a rapist. They either didn't hear me or didn't care to pay attention to the words. Soon I gave up fighting them. A part of me thinking that maybe that was helping them to get off? Helping them fire their thick load inside me... I'd grit my teeth, I'd try to relax as best as I could in such a position and I'd just let them get on with it.

On good nights it would just be one of them. Two at a push. On the bad nights...

There would be a queue and they'd all stay until each and every one of them was drained of pent-up frustrations they'd accumulated.

These weren't gay men. They were alpha-males and to them, they weren't fucking a man. They were simply *fucking*. Their eyes most likely shut as they pictured their loved ones back home waiting for them maybe? I don't know. I don't ask. I just lie there and take it until they finished with me and leave me be, wherever they haf first found me… The cell, the day room, the shower room, the utility room… I'd been fucked in all of them and - each time - left there in a puddle of my own blood and their spunk.

I've lost count of the number of times they've fucked me now and I've even lost count of the number of times I have been to the infirmary to get the ripped stitches replaced. On one such trip the warden even came and paid me a visit. He asked me to say who had done this to me but I never did. He says he can't help me if I don't speak out but - he doesn't want to help me anyway. He just wants to be seen to be doing the right thing for he knows - one day - I'll be out of here and he's probably expecting a shitstorm of bad press.

Bad press?

Who'd I tell?

I don't give him any names. Even if I did think he would do something about all of this it wouldn't change anything. Sure - a couple of them might get sent to isolation but... It's the old story of the Hydra. You cut one head off and another grows in its place. It would be the same principle here and - still - I'd find myself lying on my front in the infirmary.

*

The rapes are the worst but they're not all that I am subjected to. There are also the beatings. The days when the same group of men don't come at me with erections but rather with socks filled with whatever heavy items are hidden within. I try to defend myself as best as I can. The first time I even tried to fight back but I realised quickly that it is a pointless act. It just makes them hit harder or call for more of their friends to join in.

Easier just to take the beating.

When I do, I'm unsure as to whether they're doing it because they believe me to be a rapist or whether they're doing it out of some guilt they hold deep for having fucked me. Maybe it makes them feel better to beat on me after they use me as a fuck doll? Maybe it somehow makes them feel more masculine again, having cum inside another man's rectum.

Back in the infirmary with cuts, bruises and cracked ribs and the warden visits again and - again - he asks me who did this to me. I do not know why he bothers to visit me in here anymore. He must know by now that I won't answer him.

It will only make it worse.

*

There are very rare days in which I am left alone. They tend to be the days following a stay in the infirmary. My tormentors aren't giving me a break though. They don't give a fuck about giving me time to heal before they start the cycle again. They're leaving me be because they know I am being watched. They know the warden will be watching closely to see if anyone makes a move.

These people might be stupid enough to find themselves in here but they're not stupid enough to do anything to me whilst I am being monitored.

The days I am left alone - those rare days where I get to just lie there in pain... They're not a good time though where I get to relax and feel safe. Instead I get to lie there, my body usually throbbing, and wonder whether one of the dirty fucks has passed on any infections along with their cum and spit.

I came in here a clean man. On the quiet days I find myself lying there wondering four things... The first being - why am I even here? What did I do that was so wrong other than go home with a woman I'd met? A woman I thought liked me. The second: When were the beatings (and worse) going to start again? The third: Have I been infected with anything which will change my life for good? The fourth thing that plagues my thoughts on days where I am left alone: Will I even live to see the end of my sentence?

*

Why was she doing this to me? It was a question I wished I could have had an answer for. All I could presume was that her husband found out and it was easier to cry "rape" than to explain a one-night stand. But - even so - if only I could ask why I had deserved this? The fact she could do this to someone, put someone through this so easily...

Prisoners get visitation rights and we're permitted to write to people too although the letters we pen are subject to vetting from time to time. My family were quick to disown me, the dirty rapist. The moment the court case started they began to distance themselves. When I was found "guilty", they all but disappeared. Needless to say, I do not write to them anymore... I tried a few times, but my letters were ignored... But her... I often wonder whether she would come for a face to face if I were to write her. Invite her here... Get her to sit opposite me in the visitation room... Look her in the eye and ask her why she had done this?

I never write to her though.

For one, I'm not sure whether my letters would even get to her and - if they had - I'm not convinced she would even read them once she realised what they were... Even if she had - it wouldn't mean she'd come and see me, or even answer my question.

Another question for me to muse upon: Will I die in here without ever knowing why I was even condemned to such a place?

Part Nine
Pushing

17.

She'd set the book down as I recounted aspects of prison life she'd not been aware of previously. When I was done, we both sat there in silence. I could have said more... I could have gone into more details of the horrors I had faced, all thanks to her, but there was little point. She knew the worst of it now. She knew what she had put me through and she knew that I didn't understand why and how *that* question plagued my thoughts. It still does despite having asked her when I'd initially brought her to my home for commencement of her own sentence.

'Nothing to say then?' I asked her when I'd grown tired of the silence.

'I'm sorry,' she replied.

I couldn't help but laugh even though what she'd said wasn't *actually* funny. If anything, it was pathetic. She was sorry? Sorry for making me lose my family? Lose those years of my life? Be labelled as a rapist - something that, even if the truth came out now, would stick with me forever. Oh well, so long as she is sorry then that makes everything fucking okay.

'If I could take it back,' she went to continue but I cut her off.

'What? You'd rewind time and never spread the lies that I raped you? You'd stop me getting arrested? Stop me losing my job, my family, my life? Or you'd not have come home with me, the first time that we met?'

She went quiet a moment.

Eventually she added, 'I'd take it all back.'

'Glad to know I meant so little to you but, at the same time, I'm hardly surprised.' I looked at her, curious to know how our path had turned so dark. 'Can you at least tell me why you came back? Don't blame the alcohol either because while you were a little drunk - I *know* you weren't so drunk that you wouldn't have known what you were doing but then, we've had this conversation before.' Time and time again in fact.

'I don't know why I went back with you!'

She'd said that to me before too. Along with the excuse of being drunk, the old "I don't know why I did it" was the second most common thing she'd ever say to me and - each time she said it - it was the equivalent of finger nails down a chalk board.

'Nothing you say is going to change what happens here so why don't you just fucking tell me?' I pushed her for a truthful response. There is no way she "hadn't known" why she came back with me, just as there is no way she didn't have - in her mind - a legitimate reason for doing what she did afterwards. Maybe me reassuring her that nothing will change will get her to give me the straight answer I am sure I fucking deserve. 'Do I really not deserve to know why my life changed?'

Silence.

Always with the silence.

'You maybe think that maybe I'd treat you differently if I just had a straight answer?'

'I don't see what difference it makes!'

'You're telling me you wouldn't want to know if this was the other way around?'

'What - that I had abducted you and chained you to me.'

I looked at her with surprise on my face, unsure of what immediately to say back to that. And then...

'You want to remind yourself why you're here?'

Silence.

'Just give me the answers I'm looking for,' I pushed her again.

'I just...'

I cut her off again. 'Maybe it might help to reduce your sentence?'

She said suddenly, 'Because I was angry!'

'You reported me for rape because you were angry? Why? Because I hadn't called you? I might have done had you left me your fucking...'

She cut me off and explained, 'I went home with you because I was angry with him...'

Part Ten
Confessions

18.

I sat there dumbfounded as she explained. She'd been angry with her husband because she'd thought he was having an affair. He was being secretive, texting behind her back and then hiding his phone from her when she came over to him, or even looked in his direction. She put everything together and decided he was having an affair but instead of confronting him about it, she went out for a few drinks. The night she met me.

Her husband wasn't having an affair. He was organising a birthday surprise-trip for her and - working out the finer details - he was back and forth with her work colleagues organising time off for her. He was being a thoughtful loving husband and she feared she'd ruined it all by having - her words - a revenge fuck. In her head, he was cheating on her so it was okay for her to do the same. In reality though...

She explained that she tried to put our encounter from mind when she realised the truth of her marital situation but the guilt ate away at her and she'd find herself crying. Her husband didn't understand and tried to be there for her as best he could but - without knowing what she was crying about - he soon started to become irritated. He demanded that she either tell her what "the fuck" was going on or buck up her ideas.

... She hadn't meant to blurt out that she was raped, it just came out. Her husband was understandably shocked. He had known that she had gone out with a friend but when she hadn't come home, he had just presumed that she'd had one too many and had slept at her friend's place as it was nearer and easier to get to. She had warned him that she might do that, after all... Having already had it in her head that she was going out to fuck someone, she'd made sure she had an alibi - not that she'd care if he knew... Not if he was fucking behind her back too. Hard for him to be pissed if he was doing the same thing to her.

But he wasn't.

He had wanted to know all the details. How it had happened, where it had happened, with whom? He didn't want to leave any stone unturned and yet she said she'd just wanted to leave it and try and forget about it. He even asked if I had cum inside her apparently.

Tears streaming down her face as she explained everything to me. Did she cry when explaining it to her husband?

She had given him my address. She said that I had forced her back with him even though she had put up a fight. She had given him my name... My full fucking name. When I asked how she had known, as I'd only ever given her my Christian name, she said she had noticed it on an envelope lying on the floor by the front door.

Her husband had insisted upon the police being told. Either she went and told them what had happened or risk him being sent to prison for murder. Knowing he knew where

I lived, she felt as though she had to go to the authorities.

'I hoped there wouldn't be enough evidence to prosecute you,' she'd said to me. 'I hoped it would just have been left but you admitted to sleeping with me and... Everything snowballed...'

I'd laughed when she said that "everything snowballed". An understatement. Still, not sure why I had laughed though given the rage surging through me. I could understand why she had fucked me. I get that. I even understand her lying to try and save her marriage but - she gave him all of my details? Why not just say she had been raped, if she wanted to play that card, and make someone up? She had given him all my details! There's not a sane man in the world who'd just *leave it* when discovering the news that his partner had been sexually assaulted. They would want to murder the person responsible and - at the very least - they would want to see him rotting inside a prison cell. She could have made up a fake person but - apparently - her mind was a haze and she just didn't think...

I processed everything in my mind as she just sat there sniffling, trying to hold back the tears. I wanted to tell her to shut up but - all this time together - this is the most open she has been with me and I want to know *everything* as to why I had lost my life.

'And the baby?' I asked her eventually.

19.

'There was a baby,' she said.

Her words took me by surprise and it felt as though someone had slogged me in the gut with a heavy, clenched fist. Had I not already been sitting down, I would have fallen on my arse. *We had used protection though.*

'It was my husband's,' she added.

My heart skipped a beat and I felt my face flush with embarrassment because of my previous runaway thoughts.

'I'm sorry,' she added.

I tried to hide my embarrassment and asked, 'What happened to it?'

'I lost it.'

Her voice was quiet and her tone melancholy. It was clearly a sensitive subject. I didn't care.

'What happened to it?'

'I lost it.'

'How?'

There was a pause. She looked at me. I wondered if my expression was as cold and unsympathetic as I felt it was. Anyone else and I would feel something for them but - for her - I feel nothing. No... Not nothing. I feel as though this is karma.

She *deserved* to lose the opportunity for something good in her life for what she had done to me. She deserved this.

'I miscarried.'

'How long in?'

'Does it matter?' Her voice raised slightly. She continued but - this time - with a quieter voice, 'I lost my baby and I lost my husband... The marriage fell apart because of it. He said that whenever he looked at me he saw our dead baby. He saw your face... He saw all the negatives and none of the happiness that we once had. We tried to work on it for a while but...' She started to laugh.

'What's so funny?'

'He started to have an affair with a woman from his office. What I feared at the start - before you and me even met... That's where my marriage ended up.'

We both went quiet.

Eventually she said, 'You're not going to laugh?'

'It's not funny. Why would I laugh?'

'Thank you.'

'Thank me? No. I'm not laughing because it's not funny but don't think I feel sorry for you. I'm glad. No. I'm *fucking* glad. You ruined my life and yet you don't expect me to be happy that your life went in the shitter too? You did all of this. *All of it*. I went out for a good time that night I met you... I had a good time. I wanted it to lead somewhere else too on the strength of how I felt we connected. You went out to get revenge on your husband who was doing nothing but trying to provide for you... You fucking deserve a miserable life... You deserve all the shit that happened. You fucking asked for it...'

She was crying. She'd started halfway through my speech. I felt no guilt though. She deserved to hear how I felt. Truth be

told, I'm not sure what she was expecting...
Was she expecting me to feel sorry for her?
Was she expecting me to put my arm around
her and tell her that everything was going to
be okay?

'I actually feel sick,' I told her. 'All of
this could have been avoided had you just
tried talking to your husband. But no, you
decided to put two and two together, come
up with five and then go out to fuck
someone to get your own back... You know
how pathetic that is? How pathetic you are?
All of this could have been avoided. You
could have saved your marriage. You could
have had your baby. You could have been
happy. And - that night - I could have gone
home and just masturbated myself to sleep.
No harm, no foul. Our lives would have
continued and we'd both have been happy.
Now look at us. Look at what *you* did.'

'I really am sorry.' She added, 'Please,
just kill me. Let all of this end...'

'You really want me to kill you?'

'Yes. Please. Just kill me. I don't want to do this anymore. I don't want to do any of it anymore.'

All her words and the way she was acting now... I felt another wave of anger and bitter resentment surge through me. I jumped to my feet and shouted, 'You really want me to fucking kill you? Get the fuck up...'

Standing above her, I grabbed her by her arm and lifted her to her feet. With a tight grip on her, she let out a little squeal as I started dragging her from the room.

'What are you doing?' she asked. 'You're hurting me...'

'But that's fine,' I told her as we stumbled into the hallway, dragging the chain between us. 'You wanted me to kill you so what's a little pain with that, huh?'

I dragged her through into the kitchen and, from there, into the garage where the tools were kept. My head banging with an intensity I'd not felt since I first saw her after my release.

In the garage I threw her to the floor where she crumpled in a heap, still crying.

'You really want to fucking die?' I asked her.

I didn't want for an answer. Instead I just grabbed the axe from the array of tools I had hanging along the wall. I turned to where she was still heaped on the floor and I lifted the axe high.

She didn't even scream.

Part Eleven
Good Behaviour

20.

I dropped the axe to the floor where it landed with a loud clank of metal head on concrete ground. I looked at her, lying there on the floor where I'd thrown her. She was looking back at me with shock on her face. The chain between us - cut.

'I don't understand,' she said. There was confusion in her voice and she spoke slowly as though trying to figure out the best words to use.

'You're here because of what you did to me,' I explained. The adrenaline in my body slowing and my heart returning to its usual, and healthier, pace. 'I wanted you to be stuck in a prison for as long as I was. I wanted you to lose what you loved in life, along with your freedom…'

'You told me…'

'I know I did but you never told me everything you've just said.' I continued, 'I put you in this *prison* with me but you're already living in one.' Her own head was so much worse than anything I could put her through... The thoughts of all she'd done to her, me, her husband... Her baby... All these negative thoughts in her head. All of them are far worse than anything I could put her through. 'I'm keeping you here to teach you a lesson but... You were already living in your prison. Living with the consequences of your actions.' I added, 'All I am doing here, keeping you, is forcing myself to be locked away for another number of years when - really - I should be out there trying to rebuild the life you originally took away from me... By trying to punish you I'm just punishing myself more and - for what? You're not happy. You're not content...'

I sat on the cold concrete with the broken chain still between us. She didn't move, or even go to. The pair of us just sitting there. A broken couple, for want of a better word.

'So, what now?' she asked.

'Just go,' I told her. 'I know I have no right to ask this of you but, if you could come up with another excuse as to where you've been, I would be grateful... I mean, surely you owe me that, right? I've already served my time and...' I shrugged. 'Just do what you want... I can't stop you and I won't stop you... I just know there's little point in you being here with me.' I told her again, 'Just go.'

Slowly - seemingly unsure - she stood up.

'Really?'

I didn't answer her, nor did I move. So much time wasted with her - and because of her - and for what? So much damage to both of our lives and for what reason? This whole situation was... I frowned at her as she picked the axe up.

'What are you doing?' I asked.

She laughed and raised the axe high.

She said, 'So gullible.'

'What?'

'My husband is well. My baby will be four next month.'

'You lied to me?'

She smiled.

She swung the axe down towards…

Watch the film today!

As a "thank you" for purchasing this book, you are also able to stream the film today, for free! Just use the code below:

Code: paperbackchained2022
Entitles you to a free rent of the movie.

Code: paperbackchainedpurchase2022
Entitles you to 50% discount on the purchase.

Claim your film today from:
www.vimeo.com

For technical queries: info@purgatorypictures.co.uk

Printed in Great Britain
by Amazon